Titles in this series
I Miss You – a first look at death
My Amazing Journey – a first look at where babies come from
My Brother, My Sister and Me – a first look at sibling rivalry
My Family's Changing – a first look at family break-up
My Friends and Me – a first look at friendship
Stop Picking on Me – a first look at bullying

Text copyright © Pat Thomas 2000
Illustrations copyright © Lesley Harker 2000
First published by Hodder Wayland in 2000
This edition published in 2001

Editor: Liz Gogerly
Concept design: Kate Buxton
Design: Jean Wheeler

Published in Great Britain by Hodder Wayland, an imprint of Hodder Children's Books

A catalogue record for this book is available from the British Library.

ISBN 07500 3074 7

Printed and bound in Italy by G. Canale & C.S.p.A., Turin

Hodder Children's Books
A division of Hodder Headline Limited
338 Euston Road
London NW1 3BH

My Friends and Me

A FIRST LOOK AT FRIENDSHIP

PAT THOMAS
ILLUSTRATED BY LESLEY HARKER

HODDER
Wayland

an imprint of Hodder Children's Books

You probably know lots
of other children.

But only a few of them
are your friends.

Some people like to have lots of friends around them.

And other people like to have one or two
special friends that they play with most
of the time.

A friend can be anyone, or anything, that you enjoy being with.

It can even be someone that no one else can see!

It can be someone who you can laugh and be loud with.
Or someone you can play quietly with.

What about you?

Who are your friends? What sort of things do you do together?

Have you ever thought about what makes a good friend?

A friend is someone who you feel comfortable and safe with. It is someone who shares, and keeps their promises.

A friend tries to understand how you feel –
even if they don't feel it themselves.

It is someone who encourages you to be yourself –
even if it means being different from others.

Occasionally you might think someone is a friend – even if they are mean to you or always getting you into trouble.

But a true friend won't ask you to do things that would get you into trouble with your parents or your teachers. Anyone who does this does not deserve your friendship.

Sometimes, without meaning to, you may say or do something that hurts your friend.

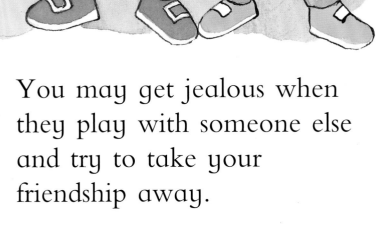

You may get jealous when they play with someone else and try to take your friendship away.

But friendship is often best when you can share it around. And with a good friend it's not so hard to say, 'I'm sorry,' when you've done something hurtful.

What about you?

Do you ever fight with your friends?
What things do you fight about?

Everybody has days when they think nobody likes them. And it isn't always easy to make friends, especially if you feel shy.

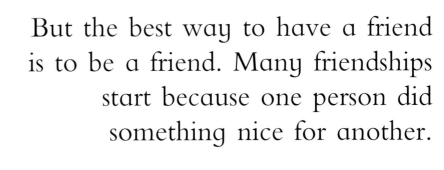

But the best way to have a friend is to be a friend. Many friendships start because one person did something nice for another.

There are lots of things in life that you don't have a choice about. You have to go to school, and brush your teeth and eat your vegetables.

But you do have a choice about which people are your friends.

Every day you will meet lots of different people. You should always try to be kind and fair to everyone you meet.

But this does not mean that you have to be friends with everyone. You can know someone and get along with them without being their friend.

What about you?

Can you think of examples of people you know who are friends and not friends? What's the difference?

23

You also have a choice about how you behave with your friends. You can choose whether to be nice or mean, whether to argue or make peace.

If you choose to do things like hitting, shouting or being rude, you may find it's a lot harder to make friends. Other people only want to be with you when you treat them well.

Having a friend and being a friend can make you feel good about yourself.

And when you feel good
about yourself, anything is possible.

HOW TO USE THIS BOOK

Friendship is one of the fundamental ways in which we begin to develop social skills such as empathy, sharing, how to appreciate the differences between people, how to express ourselves – in joy and in anger – and how to negotiate our needs in relation to the needs of others. Help your child make positive choices about their friends and about their behaviour towards their friends by encouraging positive behaviour.

Imaginary friends are very important because it is a friendship in which the child is totally in control. Children can try out lots of situations on imaginary friends and behave in ways which they couldn't with real friends. It can be hard, even frustrating, for adults to take such friends seriously, but it's a good idea to try. Allow the imaginary friend as much space in the family as you can. When your child has finished trying out this friendship, he or she will move on.

At some point your child is going to make friends with someone you don't like or who you feel is a bad influence. Childhood friendships are very complicated and intense and your disapproval may make the attraction more intense. Instead try to reinforce your child's more positive relationships. Also ask yourself what your child needs from this particular person at this particular time. Children's friendships go through many changes during these early years. Chances are with positive reinforcement of healthier relationships the change will be for the better.

As society becomes more mobile, it is very common for a friendship to end because one friend moves away. Sometimes moving away is a natural ending to a friendship and other times it is not. If your child is grieving for the loss of a friend, help them to keep in touch by letter (or if they are older by e-mail) or, if feasible, by occasional visits, while gently encouraging new friendships.

Friendship can bring lots of pleasure, but it can also bring a lot of anguish as children move in and out of each other's lives and learn how to negotiate personal boundaries and needs. Try to support your child through these difficult times rather than isolate or protect them.

Although friendship is very important in our lives, most of our training is 'on the job'. Issues about friendship are very common in school and the playground and this is a good time to get children thinking about what it means to be a friend and which people in their lives are 'friends' and 'not friends'. A good class project would be to get the entire class to produce a list of twelve ways you can be a good friend. When everyone is in agreement you can make and decorate a poster, to keep in the classroom. You can also use the list for homework, asking each child to provide examples from their own lives of how they have been a good friend.

GLOSSARY

Friendship
When you first meet someone friendship is usually just a nice feeling that you have about them. But when you have known someone a long time friendship will also be the way you act towards them. Thinking about your friend's feelings and treating them kindly are important ways to show friendship.

Jealousy
This is a feeling you have about another person. When we get jealous we are worried that another person is taking someone else's friendship, love and attention away from us. Talking to someone you trust about jealous feelings can be reassuring.

FURTHER READING

Fiction
The Velveteen Rabbit by Margery Williams
(Puffin Books, 1995)
The Selfish Giant by Oscar Wilde
(Hodder Wayland, 1996)
The Stray by Dick King-Smith (Puffin Books, 1997)
And To Think We Thought That We'd Never Be Friends by Mary Ann Hoberman
(Crown, 1999)
Are You My Friend? by Janice Derby
(Herald Press, 1993)

Non-fiction
We Can Get Along – A Child's Book of Choices
by Lauren Murphy Payne (Free Spirit, 1997)

RESOURCES

The Parents Network
Freephone: 0808 800 222
Advice on all aspects of parenting with links to local groups.

UKParents
www.ukmums.co.uk
Comprehensive website with communities where you can discuss all aspects of your children and their development with like-minded parents.